The Sea-Wave

ESSENTIAL PROSE SERIES 121

Canada Council
for the Arts

Conseil des Arts
du Canada

ONTARIO ARTS COUNCIL
CONSEIL DES ARTS DE L'ONTARIO

an Ontario government agency
un organisme du gouvernement de l'Ontario

Canadä

Guernica Editions Inc. acknowledges the support of the Canada Council
for the Arts and the Ontario Arts Council. The Ontario Arts Council
is an agency of the Government of Ontario.

We acknowledge the financial support of the Government of Canada.

The Sea-Wave

a flash novel

Rolli

GUERNICA
EDITIONS
TORONTO · BUFFALO · LANCASTER (U.K.)
2016

Michael Mirolla, general editor
David Moratto, interior and cover design
Guernica Editions Inc.
1569 Heritage Way, Oakville, (ON), Canada L6M 2Z7
2250 Military Road, Tonawanda, N.Y. 14150-6000 U.S.A.
www.guernicaeditions.com

Distributors:
University of Toronto Press Distribution,
5201 Dufferin Street, Toronto (ON), Canada M3H 5T8
Gazelle Book Services, White Cross Mills, High Town,
Lancaster LA1 4XS U.K.

First edition.
Printed in Canada.

Legal Deposit – Third Quarter
Library of Congress Catalog Card Number: 2016935359
Library and Archives Canada Cataloguing in Publication
Rolli, 1980-, author
The sea-wave / Rolli.

(Essential prose ; 121)
Issued in print and electronic formats.
ISBN 978-1-77183-053-9 (paperback).--ISBN 978-1-77183-054-6 (epub).--
ISBN 978-1-77183-055-3 (mobi)

I. Title. II. Series: Essential prose series ; 121

PS8635.O4465S42 2016   C813'.6   C2016-901518-1   C2016-901519-X

*for anyone
who has ever drowned*

Memorandum Book

When the old man stole me I remember thinking: At least I have my memorandum book. It was in the hanging pouch on the left side of my wheelchair, with some pens and raisins. In the right pouch was my new copy of *David Copperfield*. My old copy got ripped apart by shitheads.

My memorandum book is two hundred unruled pages. I filled up most of them before I was stolen, so I'm fitting things in where I can, writing everything down that I can.

The old man ... The first time he talked was along the road with the roses. He bent over and his beard brushed the top of my head. I reached up to shoo the fly but felt his dry beard.

He could be talking about himself, his own life. Or remembering something. Sometimes I mix up things that happened to me and things that happened to David Copperfield. It'll be hard, writing my autobiography.

I'm not sure he's talking to *me* but I'm writing the words down. I'm a slow writer but he speaks slowly.

I'm the old man's biographer, too.
I'm scared to death.
He's coming back.

The Sea-Wave

I hear the sea. In the deep of night, I hear it. As I lie awake, and often in ... my dreaming.

It was a prison. A kind of prison. A cell, of stone. One could hear the sea. It shattered on, the walls. Beading them with water. I could feel this, in the darkness, sliding my hand. My terror was always that the walls would *truly* shatter. That I would drown, on wet stone.

The brothers. They came and went freely. Brother Ulgoth was a dark man. His skin, an African's. When he moved through the halls — I soon knew this moving — it was ... the moving grass. His robes. I would close my eyes. I would imagine grass, beneath his black feet. I would listen, to the rushing of grass, and then his voice at the grille of the door.

"Are you comfortable?" he would ask me.

I was so seldom comfortable. I would seldom say anything but: "Yes, I am comfortable." Our ritual.

"I am so pleased," he would say.

And he would move away. I would stand there, listening. To the grass. In the wind. Imagining.

And there was brother Godslee. He came instantly and without sound. Delivering food, water. I talked with him, sometimes. We talked often. Though never … for any length. I would be speaking to him, about some small thing. About food, perhaps. And then I would ask him: "Where is this place?" Or: "What is the name, of this place?" And then he would change. His openness, would close. A curtain. He would say not a word, but turn away. He would pass me my bread, and turn away. He would slide down the hall like the crust of bread, down my throat. He would go. And I would remain. Wondering.

I was one evening, sleeping. I did not often sleep. The waves kept me awake. Sometimes I slept, for I woke one evening. There was something. The sliding, of something. A familiar something. It was … the grass.

"Are you comfortable?"

I sat up. It was not the time. It was the customary voice. It was the question. But it was not the time.

I could not answer, I did not. When a man wakes in the night, when he is suddenly woken, he feels … he is hanging. From his feet.

I said nothing. I listened, but heard nothing. It was silent. I lay down. *My imagining.*

I attempted, again, to sleep. I was nearly sleeping.

But I was again arrested, by a sound. It was the moving grass. Then a breathing, at the door. The grille. And the voice said:

"The sea-wave comes and goes forever. It rushes against everything forever. Nothing, not iron, survives it. For the sea-wave flows forever. It takes away everything, forever. All crumbs, and the phantoms of all things. Until they're nothing. Everything, we have. The good things of earth. The miserable things. All suffering. All, is salt. Your bones. They will wash away. It will take them, the wave, away. The Earth, itself, is salt, and will wash away. In the wave. For it comes and goes, forever."

I closed my eyes. I close them again, remembering.

If I Were the Leaves, I'd Be Dead

When Tay-Lin comes over, just before, I take the elevator to my room and hide. I'm not afraid of Tay-Lin, she's pretty and shy. I just don't like being around people much. I go to my room and shut the door loudly, then open it a crack and listen.

Mom must value Tay-Lin as a listener because she never shuts up in front of her. Only sometimes do I hear this leafy sound which means Tay-Lin is speaking. When Mom asks her over I know it's because she's got something on her mind and she wants to dump it onto someone else's mind. She talks about things she probably wouldn't talk about if she thought I was listening. Or if Dad was around. One time she told Tay-Lin she didn't care much for milk in tea and she never really loved my dad. She married him because it was something to do. It was an uncertain time in her life because she was having seizures. She wasn't supposed to conceive on seizure meds but god's an eccentric and she's proud she was gifted with such a beautiful child.

When she said that I shut the door and cried for a long time. When I opened it again I could just hear leaves.

Another time, Mom said how hard her life was and wondered why god was punishing her. I'm not just a wheelchair kid: I double as a kind of holy wrath.

Listening to her, overhearing her ...

It's listening to acid rain.

Circuit Sam

I had the Chatter for almost a year. It sounds like a disease; I guess it was. It was a computer. It clamped onto my armrest like a feeding tray. I pressed letters on a screen and the Chatter said them out loud in a loud voice. The voice was called Circuit Sam, a deep male voice with zero expression. Which is just how I imagined my voice sounding.

My parents loved the Chatter because it made their lives easier. It made my life a bit easier, but ...

In a bookstore, if I pressed the bathroom icon, there were icons that saved time, Circuit Sam would shout "Bathroom," and everyone would turn their heads then turn them back and pick up the book they'd just put down. Sometimes the button would stick, and Sam would just keep saying something over and over until I felt like dying.

I stopped using the Chatter. I got sick. I felt like a sick machine. My parents wanted me to keep using it, but I'd only mash the keyboard or type profanity. So they took it away. They never really got rid of it, just packed it away, like a wedding dress, hopeful.

I write notes now. It's slower, but I like it better. When you read a note in your mind, you read it — you think of it as being in a human voice, the voice of whoever wrote it. I hope that when my parents read my notes they hear the voice of a sad, bright kid who's at least trying.

They might just hear Circuit Sam.

The Loner

I like being alone but not really. Every day I wake up and think: What if Mom's dead, what if she just dropped dead? If she doesn't get me up by 7:35, I'm sure she's dead. I lie there under a thought bubble of her on the floor with a broken jam jar and a broken head. A closet shutting means she's collapsing. Then she comes in the door, and it's okay to hate her again.

I'm a loner. It's just easy. It protects me. It's safe in my room. I read books, I'm a bookmark. You don't get loved but you don't get hurt either by people you love, which hurts more than anything. It's easier to hate people the way they hate millionaires, they'll never be one. I'm alive, I have a skeleton, but I'll just never be a real kid or feel like a real human being.

When people see me they feel sad. They might smile sadly. I shake up their moral centres. I wreck their shopping day. There are people who do that even to me.

I *hate* being one of those people. I can't just hide all day though I sometimes want to. I sometimes do. I'm trading happy for not being the wrecking ball and the house it's wrecking. I can do that for people, at least.

It's not much.

It's something.

Murder

I didn't *see* who stole me, not for hours. Not till we were out of the city.

I pictured — in the bubble above my head was a pudgy guy with glasses and acne, floating in sweat, who filled the whole bubble.

The guy who walked in front of me when my chair stopped moving and climbed down the riverbank and knelt down ...

He was just a frail old man. A stick man, who pricked the bubble.

The old man knelt down and looked at the water, at his *reflection* in the water, I'm guessing. Like Narcissus only old and puzzled. He didn't drink at all, just stared.

When he got up, I closed my eyes. I'm not sure why. I didn't open them until he was back behind me, and we were moving again.

I think if he was going to murder me or hurt me ...

He'd've done it a long time ago.

Right?

Writing

My memorandum book was a gift from my cousin the writer. At first I thought it was cheap because I'd've rather had a real book. But then I thought it probably would've been one of *her* books, so I was lucky. I threw the memorandum book in my desk drawer. But one time when I was just so angry I couldn't read I took it back out and started writing in it. Writing is hard for me, it takes a long time, but I'm getting better. It helps with my anger. My sadness.

My cousin said all kinds of family drama winds up in her books, and since no one reads them, no one finds out. She still gets invited to the BBQs, and gets handshakes from the people she said were bullshitters. Writing is a kind of minor revenge, like stealing the left slipper of someone who stabbed you in the neck, which I guess to her makes it worthwhile. Personally …

I haven't decided yet.

The Angel Lady

Our daughter vanished.

The woman looked pretty normal. She had long hair even though she was over forty. She had a brittle voice that made you listen carefully in case you dropped it.

She was a beautiful, healthy girl. And she vanished.

The whole time she spoke to us she didn't blink. The trick to not crying might be to dry out your eyes.

She was a prostitute. She got into hard drugs.

I have to admit that sort of made her less angelic in my book. I was picturing Little Dorrit or something. I'm pretty judgmental.

We found her in the Parliamentary Gardens. In a rose bush. Bleeding. They were actually white roses.

Even my teacher swallowed hard. I stared at her like, Where do you find these people? She stared at a square on the floor.

My daughter is an angel. She speaks to me. She hovers above me, and guides me. She forgives me. She loves me.

Without really realizing it, I think the whole class looked up at the ceiling. All I could see was the curved mirror they put in after the shootings. In her warped back reflection the woman's shoulders were a bit like folded-back wings.

I looked at my teacher again. She started clapping.

I guess it was over.

I Have No Friends

I have no friends. It just isn't possible. It would take a pretty weird kid to touch me and murder their social life forever. Life is tough. It might be even tougher without friends. So what.

Every Saturday, my mom or dad takes me to the park. We sit by the water and feed the birds. One time half my class walked by, going wherever kids go. They looked at me, and not one of them smiled or said hi. But then one girl, the new girl, looked back and laughed. Then they all looked back and laughed. I squeezed my bread bag until the crumbs were just dust. I felt like the dust rattling in the bag.

I closed my eyes hard. Then my mom said: "Jealous. They are all just jealous." That's her word, that's always the word for children who are broken. I'm not sure she even understands it. Because when you're not pretty or popular, and there isn't even a chance of having talent, what could they be jealous of, Mom? You never really think.

There's a tree in the park that's the one thing I like. It's just a perfect small tree that's by itself. I like to sit under it in my chair and read. Or sometimes my dad lifts me and sits me on the grass. I want to be buried under that tree. Only I've never told anyone.

I Have a Giant Uncle Who's a Refrigerator

I have a giant uncle who's a refrigerator or bigger. If he was really a house someone from the city would hammer a note into his forehead saying he was scheduled for demolition and please keep out. His tongue is either swollen or it sounds like he's eating it. He can still walk but only so fast that if you don't stop him he'll walk into walls. He's like a remote control man and someone is having fun with the controls. I can't really understand him but what he's saying sounds like "I wish I was dead."

My giant uncle reminds me of me. At Christmas people say hi but then they wheel me into a corner and ignore me. After maybe an hour they deposit my giant uncle in another corner, in an armchair, and we just sit there staring at each other. Once in a while my auntie will come into the room to yell "No juice!" or "Not the green pill!" Her treatment of him is shit, though it's not like anyone says anything. Not even when she says: "I'd love to play this hand, but I have to change his *stupid* diaper," and flings herself out of the kitchen. And he is so not beyond being able to hear and understand her, but he is definitely beyond crying anymore. Me too.

The Whale with the Harpoon Earrings

I'm quiet and still and the trouble with being quiet and still is that people will occasionally mistake you for a toilet. It's easy to take things out on me or blame me. Mom does this pretty much daily. She used to love me. She's like the dolls with the smaller dolls in them, but she forgets they're there, that one of those moms really loved me. Or she could never *hurt* me. I'm a different kid now, too. But I still remember the smaller kid, in her sarcophagus, who loved her mom and felt loved. I still feel her, sometimes. Life would be easier ...

Occasionally my dad stands up and whispers to Mom not to say this or that in front of me but it doesn't matter. I can hear her from the kitchen. I can hear *him*. He doesn't talk much about me so I have to listen.

What are we going to do with her? What will happen to her? What's ... going ... to happen?

Then I'm swallowing water and sinking. I'm listening and I'm sinking. I'm the whale with the harpoon earrings. Sinking.

When my parents are suddenly alone I go straight to my room but the elevator doors don't always close fast enough. Or they open and drop me in the middle of something, a storm cloud I thought was a pillow. I listen and I watch my parents roll out of the kitchen like smoke, looking only at the space exactly above me or beside me. Then I look at *them* sinking down in the two big couches and I think: What have I done to these people?

I'll bet they ask themselves the same thing.

The Roses

When I closed my eyes, it was night. When I opened them ...

We were going down a dirt road. There were roses growing alongside it, wild ones. I could smell them.

The sun was shining. The *sky*. You don't see much of it, in the city.

There wasn't a building of any kind in miles.

I've been to other cities but I've never been *out* of the city. Parks are half cement. They're busier than streets.

The old man was quiet for once. The way his beard moved, I could tell he was looking around. Maybe enjoying himself, a little. He slowed down a little.

I could only smell roses.

I pictured the skyscrapers behind us, fading away.

My future was fading away.

I was still scared, but ...

The roses.

I hadn't felt that happy or relaxed in a long time.

The Sea-Wave II

In such a prison, if a man passed through the hall, and moved the air, it moved on no other occasion. In the warm season ... I would hear feet, and rush to the grille, as the man in the cell across the hall. Breathing and breathing the wind. Then waiting, till the next man passed.

I was reading, one book that remained. The light from the grille was sufficient. It should not have been. But I had so grown accustomed, to the missing light. As ... a fish. Of the deep sea.

I was slowly reading. One page, and the facing page, perhaps, per hour.

I finished a page. I raised a finger, to turn it. *It turned itself.*

I rose. I closed my hands on the bars of the grille. *What man, thinking, moving, could produce this wind?* There had never been such wind. Stirring, even, my hair. Blowing down my throat.

I stood, looking. The man across the hall, through bars, looked also. For the man.

But there was no one. No man. This blowing seemed to come ... from above. As a letter. Warm, and feeling. From one beyond the prison. It could not have come from within.

I breathed in. I had not breathed so deeply for so long. The other man breathed. I could hear him, even, with my own eyes closed, breathing in. Listening. To the wind. And the pages, in the wind. Turning and turning.

We groaned, both, in sadness. As it passed away.

Tan

I'm getting a really good tan.

Writer

I'm sad about my future, I worry about it. But a writer is something I could be. It would be a job but also a way of communicating, feeling emotion, being more like people. I don't mean being *like* them ... I just mean feeling real.

My fear is that, as a writer who's also a wheeler, a wheelchair person, people would just pat me on my hair and say I was beautiful and way to go. I'd be that heartbreaking kid in the framed article in the *Sunday Sun*. People wouldn't judge me or ignore me or laugh, which my cousin says happens constantly and only makes you a better writer.

The last thing I'd want to be is a mediocre writer.

There's already a million of those.

Autobio

It's tough, writing about yourself. Your veins are barbed wire and you're pulling them out. Or you're playing a guitar but then thorns grow on the strings and you have to keep playing because everyone's watching.

I'm not remembering nice things, I haven't had a nice life. I'm picking onions out of my salad and just staring at a plate full of onions. I write a bit, then I feel like crying.

Before I started writing, though ...

I don't ever want to remember what that feels like.

Disneyland

I went to Hell but it was Disneyland.

At a school assembly, the principal called me forward. Someone pushed me forward. Someone in a Mickey Mouse suit came out of the bathroom. As he put his arms around me — I am terrified of mascots, the principal said I'd love it at Disneyland. Then he hugged me, too.

My parents appeared. They put their arms on the pile. They looked so happy. When a sick kid wins a prize ... I wondered if I was dying.

When we finally got to Disneyland, my parents fought the whole way, I couldn't go on most of the rides because they weren't "equipped for my needs."

We ate corn dogs and took pictures.

Before I could stop him, Donald Duck squeezed me and as I screamed inside, Dad snapped a photo. It hung on the living room wall for years until I knocked it down with a broom and pushed it deep in the trash. There's still a blank space on the wall. No one's said anything.

We haven't been on vacation since.

François' Cathedral

W

e were in a dried up pasture. My legs were getting scratched up pretty bad by cactuses. I saw a brick building in the distance. The old man must've noticed it too because he turned me towards it and pushed me as fast as he could.

It was a house — once. It had three walls and no roof, like a diorama. Teenagers had partied in it. "*François'* Cathedral" was spray-painted on the one wall. "Becky is a whore" was spray-painted on the other.

The old man walked through the door hole, there was no door, and around the house.

The floor was rotten in places. I was afraid — I thought he might fall through the floor. But instead, he went batshit.

He picked up a part of a bedframe and hit the walls with it. He kicked them. Whatever he could get his hands on, he threw it. He threw bricks. He threw *himself.* He knocked down the one wall just by ramming into it.

The old man didn't calm down until the last wall

had fallen. Then he sat in a rotten armchair with his head in his hands, panting.

I remember thinking: What the fuck is wrong with this guy?

Coral

My fat aunt Coral is a riot and a lousy person. She is just so pink and fat. She laughs too much, and wears too much enormous jewellery. She's like a pig on a pearl leash sniffing out gossip then trotting up to your table and vomiting. I like her gossip because it's malicious and it's nice to know who's dying. She is shallow and destructive.

My dad and Coral are siblings but don't talk much. When she comes over he likes to say hi then take a nap or run errands. Then Coral will put her feet up and talk to my mom for hours.

I typically avoid my family but with Aunt Coral I don't mind hanging around and listening. It's great listening to people gossip because it's the one time they mean what they're saying. It has to be a huge relief to people. Aunt Coral likes to kick off her tight shoes — it probably feels like that. She gets so comfortable, it's like she's lounging on her skeleton. And then she says the most shocking things about everyone I ever heard of, and never stops smiling.

I like Aunt Coral. She talks to me without changing her voice, like I'm an everyday person. She even talks to me when other people have left the room. That's a small thing, but it means a lot.

One time she told just me that her one daughter wasn't even her husband's daughter, but just from some fling with the butcher. I thought: Why are you telling me this? But I guess she needed to tell *someone* and figured I was a pretty safe bet for discretion.

The last time I saw Coral she was fifty pounds heavier than the time before. She wheezed just coming up the front steps, and right away sat down. She doesn't leave her house much now but sits in her armchair with the phone in her hand. "I tell people the truth," she told my mom once, "but I tell my telephone *everything*." All day she sits there soaking up gossip and getting fatter and fatter. She needs a cane now from the knee strain, and will probably be in a wheelchair one day. I'm kind of looking forward to it.

Shit

The day I fell down the stairs ...

Mom asked me if I was okay staying home by myself for an hour or two while she went to the dentist, and I of course said yes. I was initially supposed to go along but she was running behind. She took me to the bathroom then took off.

I thought I'd watch a movie. So I wheeled towards the elevator, which is right at the top of the stairs. I pressed down hard on the forward button on the directional pad. Pressing harder doesn't make me go any faster, it's just impertinence. Once in a while, though, pressing too hard makes the button stick. Which is just what happened. Sometimes I can unstick the button, but there wasn't time, there's maybe two feet between the elevator and the staircase. I didn't have time to panic even, just to brace myself as that top step got closer and I shot over it.

I didn't instantly fly out of my chair or anything, I bumped violently but held on tight. For a while I thought I'd be okay, I'd just thump on down in my chair then cruise across the floor till I stopped. Another possibility: I might stop half-way down on the landing and have to wait there like it was an ice floe till someone rescued me.

Neither of those things happened. Just before I got to the landing, I flew out of my chair, I couldn't hold on. I did a hard somersault where my neck almost snapped before my body flew over top of it. Then I slid down on my back, hit my butt hard and became airborne. I landed with a loud click on my face on the hardwood floor. My glasses broke in half. Then my wheelchair landed on my back.

I lay there in a pile waiting for my mom to come home and put me together again. I could see the clock on the cable box. An hour passed. Two. *Three.* I held on as long as I could. Then I shit my pants.

It got dark. Still no Mom. At six, Dad came home from work. He put his coat on the coat rack, and flicked on the light. When he saw me lying there, he said: "Shit."

He was right.

Dandruff

The old man has dandruff. When he wheels me over a rough patch, it snows. My glasses are blanketed with skin cells.

"To scratch an itch," said the narrator of a nature documentary, "is one of nature's greatest pleasures." Well, I might feel an itch, a wicked itch on my leg or something, my back, but there's nothing I can do. When you ignore an itch it only gets more powerful. Like North Korea. Or it floats all over me, this lilypad of itchiness, up and down my body and I scream internally. When it finally passes there's a kind of mild relief which is probably not even close to as good as you'd feel from scratching.

I don't have dandruff. It would be worth having dandruff, though, if I could only scratch it. I can touch my head, but ...

Life is quite a bit worse than a nature documentary.

Major Depression

Mom has major depression. "I have major depression today," she'll say, like it's a headache, and take Aspirin.

She goes to Dr. Blignaut twice a week but she goes to me two or three times a day to complain about her major depression. She has no energy, she says, it's a labour of Hercules to even make toast. "I wish I was dead," she'll say, but I have difficulty believing this because if she was dead she'd have no one to complain to.

Dad works twelve hours a day and when he's not working he's running long errands. He could be having an affair. When he *is* home, he opens a newspaper and holds still for two or three hours. Mom looks for him but it's too late because his skin has changed to the colour of newsprint. So she hunts me down, instead.

It's depressing.

Bacon Bones

The only kid I ever identified with was Bacon Bones. His head was too big. He went from being a shy, big-headed kid to a total shithead. He got bullied so much about his big head that he hurt too much for just one kid and needed to hurt other kids. But he never hurt me. He even once defended me from people. I guess I was the one kid he identified with.

Too bad he's in prison.

The Sea-Wave III

It was not a dream.

The wave came *in*. I was sleeping. I leaped up. My *hands*. I felt the cold water, pouring.

I felt on the wall, for the hole. It was only very small. I thought to grab something ... but there was nothing. So cold, the water, on my throat.

I folded my hands. I pressed them on the hole. But still, it poured water. *Stop. God.* My hands pressed together, as in prayer.

I could hold no more.

I cried out.

Someone opened the door.

Odour Coat

I miss the smell of people. The old man has a smell but it's just the one smell and not a good one. If you put maybe ten people together, there's just instantly this smell, sort of like how whatever's in garbage smells like garbage. I miss that people smell where there's sweat and perfume and whatever and it gets painted on your skin and taken with you like an odour coat. I tried smelling my sleeve to see if I still smelled like my house, like *people*, but I didn't. I smelled cold, and strange. Which is pretty much how I felt.

Bickersteeth

There was an ancient guy at the public library, maybe eighty-nine, ninety. He *worked* for the library, barely. He gathered stray books from cubicles and slept in them. The squealing book cart was his walker.

His name was Bickersteeth.

I heard this conversation a lot:

"Who *is* that?" someone would ask the reference lady, nodding in Bickersteeth's direction.

"Bickersteeth," she'd say, without even looking.

"Bickersteeth, eh? Like something out of Dickens?"

The reference lady would grimace or grin, depending on the time of day.

"Why doesn't he retire?"

The reference lady would either grit her teeth or grimace and say:

"We can't make him."

Apparently Bickersteeth was hired by the library when it was still being built. The contracts back then said you couldn't be forced to retire but when the time came most people were overjoyed to get out of the public library. Not Bickersteeth.

I was reading one day in the cubicle no one walks by. I heard a squealing and a diapery sound and looked up. Bickersteeth was standing over me.

"Are these *your* books?" he said in the shyest voice, pointing at a stack at my elbow. They were contemporary poetry so I emphatically shook my head.

Bickersteeth kept one palm on the cart for support and picked the books up one by one with his other trembling hand. Then he grabbed hold of the cart with both hands again reverently.

He breathed deeply.

He closed his eyes.

He shit himself. No doubt about it.

Once he finished, he kept moving. The diapery sound and the squealing got quieter and quieter.

I wheeled to the bathroom as quick as I could and threw up.

On my way out, passing the reference desk ...

"Bickersteeth, eh? Almost Dickensian."

The reference lady grimaced.

Bickersteeth *does* sound Dickensian. But no one in Dickens shits themselves, not even Mrs. Clennam. A real Victorian holds it. Even if it kills you.

Maybe a month later, at my cubicle, I saw a new teen with a shiny cart. Then I looked and saw Bickersteeth's empty cart against the wall, like Tiny Tim's crutch.

I don't know why. But I felt like crying.

library

I got tired of waiting for Dad, so I tried getting a book out of my backpack. When people see me struggling, it offends me if they try to help because I'm not a vegetable. It offends me even more if they walk past without offering.

If I'm bored enough, I picture a younger woman in a skirt who walks up with a mildly concerned face but then stops just short of me, smiles in a "boy, did I underestimate her" kind of way, then turns and walks off, smoothing her skirt and smiling in a way that can only mean pride and kindness.

That's the best case scenario.

It hasn't happened yet.

Chad

When the teachers want a longer smoke break, they drag in a motivational speaker. Last year we were in the gym waiting, there was a squealing like a wheelchair and this tiny smiling woman wheeled up to the lowest setting on the mic stand. When a hundred kids gasp, it's an ocean. She waited for it to die down then she said, smiling:

"I do not feel ashamed or isolate myself. I live in my own apartment and drive an adapted van. I am physically active. I'm on a rowing team. I steer the boat."

She went on talking, I wanted to get away, I couldn't stop staring. She looked like she was missing half her bones. She had Brittle Bone Disease. I couldn't breathe. It was so depressing listening to her. I felt so pathetic. When she got to the part about her boyfriend ... The history teacher started crying. She could've been teaching me about evil Germans but instead she was letting me sit there and be emotionally cut to pieces.

The laziness and stupidity of teachers is easily the most destructive thing in a child's life. One time our science teacher instead of teaching us put on this video about genetic disorders and played with his phone for an hour. There was a segment about Down Syndrome, and exactly what happens to your body and brain, and Chad, who sat across from and behind me, just burst out crying and said: "That's *me*." We all knew he had Down Syndrome. But I guess no one had ever told him. I wanted to pick the TV up and throw it out the window. Mr. Ed just kept playing with his phone. Chad cried all morning. He's never really been the same.

Anything

I would do anything to forget what the old lady said to the old lady.

Isn't that sad? Doesn't that just break your heart? It breaks my heart that people are so stupid and selfish they'd keep a child like that alive. Just look at the poor thing suffering. She doesn't even stand a chance.

I would do anything to forget.

Blue Magnitude

I love most kinds of music but I need jazz to live.

My favourite group is Blue Magnitude. When I'm depressed, when I'm *more* depressed than usual, I'll put on Blue Magnitude, turn it up, and just close my eyes and listen without thinking for as long as I can. Because it's only a matter of time before Mom will open the door and say: "How can you listen to that depressing crap?" and turn it down or off, not realizing she's turning *me* down or off, or not caring. Or she'll put on some oldies instead and say: "Now that's happiness," but it's like cheerleaders bearing a casket and the instant she leaves I throw the lid open and they skip off.

Blue Magnitude *is* depressing but life is depressing and it's the right kind of fabric to patch me up. It's camouflage. When I listen to jazz, I disappear. I'm not suffering; I'm not there.

I listen to music every day. If I couldn't ...

I'd die.

Emotion

I cry sometimes, though not from sadness. Mostly my crying is anger. It isn't vocal crying, I can't produce tears, but the emotion is the thing, right? I have so much emotion.

The best thing about my crying is that I can do it anywhere and no one can tell. I don't have to inflate myself into a bigger spectacle.

I could cry all day and no one would know.

I sometimes do.

Hazy and lost

The old man stopped. I could hear him — he walked in front of me. He was staggering around like the world was new. His chest was going up and down.

When he turned and he looked at me ...

His *eyes*. They were so bright. Not hazy and lost like usual. Bright and clear.

He looked at me and he took a step back. He took a second step and banged into a tree.

Then he stood there with his back against a tree, breathing hard with his eyes closed, for a long time.

His breathing slowed down.

He opened his eyes.

Hazy and lost. As usual.

He wiped his nose on his arm and got back behind me.

We kept moving.

Gyokuro

Tay-Lin gave me a box of gyokuro tea. She gave it to my mom but said it was a gift for me. This surprised me because I'd never actually met Tay-Lin. She might've seen me wheeling out of the room, or getting into the elevator.

When I opened the box there was a note that read: "This is gyokuro, a relaxation tea. It's something that's helped me a lot. Tay-Lin."

She *knew*. She barely knew me, but she knew.

I have panic attacks. I've never told anyone. My parents don't know.

Tay-Lin *knew*.

I used up all the gyokuro. It really did help.

I wish I had more.

The Credits

He was facing me, the old man, he was over top of me. I could only see his face. It was raining, there was no shelter, I think maybe he was trying to shelter me. His face was as big as a movie screen.

One big pearl of water ran down his forehead, nose, around his lips, into his beard, then down off a long curling hair right into my mouth and down my throat.

This is real.

It's a movie but it's real.

The credits are piling up at my feet.

This is really happening.

The Sea-Wave IV

The *tones* of the sea, are so many. It is not one animal.
It is *so many*. It can be, and it was so often, the deepest
tone. The conversation of one thing, and another, more
ancient, and greater. *Imagining them.* I could see them
... beyond, the wall. I could picture them, and it would
not even be imagination. But ... a puzzling-together, of
perception. As one assembling, with closed eyes, the
bones of someone speaking. Some incredible skeleton.
If it should brush the wall, this animal ... I would go so
far, as to wonder.

Yet often, and more often, the tone was not so. It
was little more than water. The tunnelling through
water, of one fish. The *murmur.* Or a million fish,
together. In their freedom, teeming, and so very near
... one who was not free. The still prisoner of a stone
aquarium. Who could float, only, as a fish in glass. And
listen. And *listen.*

Leaves

I could hear the ocean.

When I opened my eyes, I saw trees.

We weren't moving, I couldn't see the old man, I was worried he'd abandoned me. I imagined a coyote jogging off with my femur. Even if it wasn't healthy.

I pressed forward on my control pad. The wheels just threw up dust. The motor wasn't designed for off-road use. You have to charge the battery every day, too, which wasn't happening.

I felt panicky and giddy. I kept telling myself I wasn't alone, that any minute now I'd feel the chair start moving and the familiar beard hairs rubbing the top of my head.

But after five, ten minutes, nothing. Twenty minutes. I tried turning my head very slowly to the left, like I was doing my exercises, then to the right, as far as I could, which is only an inch or two, on a good day. But there was no sign of him. No sound, either, except that ocean sound of the wind in the leaves.

Then I saw a face. A *reflection*. On the inside of my glasses.

It was the old man. Frozen. He was on his knees. The branches were jumping all around him, it was windy, but he was as still as a tree trunk. Covering his ears. And the look on his face ...

He looked terrified.

Smart

If I have a talent, if it counts, it's that I'm smart. I *became* smart. I was just a dumb kid until I started reading. Not just dumb kid books, but books nobody even looked at or knew existed. If you read a book and you understand it all the way through, it's probably not doing much for your brain.

I read Dickens pretty early on. The first time I read *A Tale of Two Cities* I maybe understood fifty words of it. I understood every dull word of *Chuzzlewit*. *David Copperfield*, though, is the best thing I've ever read. Reading anything else is a disappointment. I'd rather be illiterate than not read *David Copperfield*. Most people are illiterate. Because if you *don't* read good books, or you *can't* read good books, either way, you're not reading good books. Most people don't realize they can't actually read.

I read good books, I became smarter, I became un-happy. Probably lots of people do. Knowing more just makes you sadder. Maybe I could still be that happy-go-lucky kid in a wheelchair, trying hard to smile, if I really tried.

Sorry Mom and Dad. I'd rather read *David Copperfield*.

Soft Room

Okay.

One time I was wheeling down the hallway at the Rehabilitation Centre, waiting for my dad to pick me up. He usually goes for coffee across the street till I'm finished my exercises.

There was an open door that's normally closed. I went through it down another hallway that was darker. I turned once, and just before the second turn I saw one half of a long glowing window in the wall that went down almost to the floor. There were a man and woman standing in front of the window, looking through it. They seemed pretty worried and caring like parents. As I moved closer I could see more of the window, and a man in a lab coat standing beside an empty wheelchair. He was looking through the window too and sometimes writing something on a clip-board.

This was all none of my business, but I was curious. I went closer. The people didn't seem to notice me. They were talking in quiet voices. I just wheeled up quietly behind them until I could see through the window, too.

It was a big white room. The walls and floor were white foam. There was a guy, maybe ten years older than me, with a beard, on the floor. He was rolling on the floor groaning. That was all he could do. If he came to a wall he just kicked it or flailed against it. Then he rolled the other way.

The mother said: "I really think this will help with his rage."

Then she waited a while and said slowly: "If only he'd had this when he was younger. He really could've used this. Things would've been ... so different."

The father shook his head. Then he said, quietly: "No. They wouldn't've, Helen. They wouldn't've one bit."

Then the man with the clipboard looked at me. He was about to say something, I think, but I just kept going around the corner like I had somewhere to go. Also, I felt sick to my stomach and wanted to at least get to a water fountain.

The empty wheelchair was sitting next to a door. As I passed by it I looked up. The sign on the door read: "Soft Room."

I've always thought I'd be a happier kid if I'd never seen the Soft Room.

In Dickens

If I lived in Dickens, my name would be Cripplewitch.
I love Dickens but what I don't get is that if your name
is your major character flaw why someone would still
marry a Murdstone, or trust a Krook. If he was trying
to say that people are just dumb, he's kind of stating
the obvious. But it must've been a riot, being this wiz-
ard who could turn anyone who irked him into a Peck-
sniff or a Barnacle. It was kind of like word murder;
he was Dickens the Ripper. If you're observant and
super-popular, you can actually do a lot of damage. I'm
pretty observant, too. Once I lost twenty pounds before
anyone noticed, and that was a waitress. I think if I
spontaneously combusted my mom would keep talking to the ashes as she dusted the living room. Then
she'd sweep me up and wonder what happened to me.

If my mom lived in Dickens, her name would be
Oblivia Grimsack.

Pessimism

One night I woke up, I was so dizzy. We were in the middle of nowhere. It was raining. I was sick and so dizzy. It was — I imagine it's what being on drugs is like. I counted the stars, but then I realized, with the rain, I shouldn't even really be able to see any stars. Then I couldn't see any.

I guess that's pessimism.

The Leaning Tower

I love books but I was once murdered by books just about.

I call the white bookcase in my room The Leaning Tower. It's where I keep English Literature, including all my Dickens. I have everything by Dickens except *Chuzzlewit*, which I threw out the window.

At first the white bookcase didn't lean, but as I added more books it started leaning. I tried putting the heavier books on the bottom shelf but over time, I just needed the space. I don't do paperbacks, I kept putting hardcovers higher and higher. That made the tilting worse but after reaching the one o'clock position the bookcase basically stabilized. So I stopped thinking about it.

Then one day I was in my room reading, and a book fell over my shoulder, onto my lap, then a hundred more. Then the top shelf of the bookcase stabbed me in the back of the neck. My angry head now occupied the top shelf space, like a bust of Beethoven. I realized I was the vertical part of an acute triangle, and in acute pain. Also, if I pressed forward on my directional pad, all that would happen would be that my head would keep bending back, the top of the bookcase would scrape up my forehead and possibly my head would snap off. So I decided to just wait there till my mom found me. Which wasn't too long because of the loud sound of all the books falling.

My mom helped me put the books back on the shelves. The way we arranged them the bookcase didn't tilt as bad; it hasn't fallen since. I still have a mark like a birthmark on my neck.

The first book that fell on my lap was *Martin Chuzzlewit*. That's partially why I threw it out the window.

Anxiety

When my anxiety gets the better of me it's like my nerve cells are doing hard arithmetic. I think of them holding pencils and checking the clock. I can't wring my hands, I wring the inside of my stomach like it's a hateful dog. Or I try my breathing. I learned these breathing tips on TV, though they don't generally work. I basically just have to wait. It's like, if a prince spills hot soup on you, you have to just grin till your skin stops burning.

It's hell.

Goliath

My parents went to church before I was born. They got married in a church.

If a ninety-pound kid can kill god, god can't be up to much.

I'm the kid with the slingshot.

Angry

get angry. When I get angry I can't control my anger. It won't burn out. I don't know if that means there's something wrong with me or it's just because of my life, I have a lot of compressed rage. My throat feels like fire climbing a ladder. I suffer. I can't go for a run, I can't make it go away.

I hate my anger. But I just can't *do* anything.

Will you help me please because I'm stuck?

Thunderstorm

It was storming and we were going really fast downhill. There was a river at the bottom of the hill and some trees. I was soaked. My glasses were soaked; I could barely see.

I wondered how the old man could run so fast. Then I heard something that was like far-away screaming. Oh god, I thought. It's happening. I've gotten away. I'm rocketing down a steep hill, into deep water. My nightmare.

My teeth were rattling, so I pressed them hard together. I squeezed my armrests. That was the wrong thing to do. I should've tried to fall off my chair as soon as possible, and let it drown. But I was scared of falling off, I was going so fast. The rain made it confusing.

I hit something, the wheelchair hit something. The chair stayed still but I went flying. I'm not a god type but I remember thinking god don't let me fall in the river and drown.

Then I fell in the river.

Water flowed into me like I was the Titanic. I choked. I just about blacked out, but then I was in pain because someone grabbed me by the hair and pulled me up out of the water.

The old man was crying. He hugged me but didn't say anything and put me back in my chair. Then he pushed me back up the hill. The whole time he pushed me, he was crying. Eventually he stopped crying. It stopped raining, too.

I just about died.

The Sea-Wave V

There was in one corner of the floor, a hole. The *sewer*. Though it soured what little there was of air, from such a place came something ... wonderful.

Singing. The brothers, singing. In some hidden chamber. It seemed ... there were not even words to their hymn, but emotion, only. As if they fingered the strings ... of emotion. And whichever they touched, touched *me*.

I could only listen. The singing. It was a very great wave. Taking ... me. A sea-star, on the dark waters. Its mystery. Though sorrowful, so wonderful. In tone so beautiful. They must have been singing, the men, in some cavern of stone. Echoing, as several thousand men. Down corridors. In dark corners. From pipework emerging. As a tone, from an organ.

It was ... holy. Their sorrow. It was in itself religion. Their *emotion*. It could have been my own ... emotion. Then. Listening. Bowing over, the hole.

My tears fell into the very sound of singing.

Don't Talk

Don't talk to me. Because you never really talk to me. You talk over me, around me, down to me, through me, but never *to* me. Your words go through me, like x-rays, without sticking to me, because they were never meant for me, but for the people standing next to me. The pharmacist and his wife are really keen to see what doting parents are like in the face of adversity, and I'm so glad you have the extra time to show them. To demonstrate. You have hardly any time for me, but you at least have time for somebody. And that just makes me so happy.

I am *so* happy.

Just don't ever talk to me again.

My Devices

My parents took me to Dr. Fritz, a prosthetist. He went on about devices, what great, great devices they had these days, and wouldn't I be so much happier and more complete if I owned one or more of these devices? He faced me and his words hit me in the face, but his eyes were always stuck on my parents. He talked in a fake-ly gentle way about his devices, rubbing his hands along them like he was selling reams of the finest silk, only it was Arm Buddies or the Motorized Claw. He did these demonstrations where he'd first try to pick up a glass of water, pretending I guess he was a typical spastic kid, *without* the aid of a device, and, of course, knocking it onto the floor. Then he'd strap on an Arm Buddy and lift and drink the whole glass down, not spilling a drop. And I'd be sitting there grinding my teeth in silence. One of my other doctors told my parents that teeth-grinding was a sign of a vitamin deficiency. They gave me magnesium powder, though it didn't work. That should've been their first clue.

In the end my parents broke down and ordered a pair of Arm Buddies *plus* a Motorized Claw Petite, which is the smaller model. It was maybe two months before they were ready because they had to be custom-moulded. The day the call came, my parents were so nervous, it made me nervous. Dr. Fritz strapped on the left Arm Buddy, then the right one. He attached the Motorized Claw Petite to the extension port on the Arm Buddy on my right arm, which he decided was my dominant arm. Then he wheeled me in front of the mirror and waved my parents over.

I looked at myself in the mirror. My parents ... They looked like raisins, or dried up and defeated. Which is basically how I felt. Dr. Fritz asked me to go ahead and try picking up a stuffed rabbit, which I could keep, and as I closed the claw around its head I remember thinking: I am the claw game.

I actually cried that day. There was a bit of moisture. I didn't think I could ever really cry.

After a month or two, I gave up on my devices. Because I can grip things fine myself, I've improved, just squeezing thick things is difficult. I can hold a pen or a pencil fine. I don't think I'll ever make orange juice.

My devices helped a little with certain things. They

weren't worth it. It's not worth feeling like you take batteries, even if life is 10% easier. Because I'd rather it was tough. I'd rather it was just so horribly tough, and I was just a little less pathetic.

I guess it's my dream.

Jaycee

My dad watches the news and reads the newspaper at the same time. If something on TV really interests him, he lowers his newspaper for a minute, then goes back to reading. One night, my dad lowered his newspaper, then he folded it up and set it on his lap. This made me curious so I set down *David Copperfield*.

There was a wheelchair girl on TV wearing a birthday hat. It was just some fuzzy old footage. Then they showed an older man in handcuffs being taken into the court house. Her father. He'd smothered her. He claimed she was suffering and didn't want to be alive so he euthanized her. He was just a farmer, he said, not a criminal. His daughter wanted to die, she didn't tell him this, she couldn't communicate, but he just knew it. She had to take morphine, so he gave her all of it.

They showed the footage of the girl again. She was thin and opened her mouth a lot. She looked like me. Someone, probably her mother, held a cake in front of her, then blew the candles out for her. The girl just kept opening and closing her mouth. I couldn't tell if she looked happy or sad.

I looked over at my dad and he turned his head away from me quickly and picked up his newspaper. Then he disappeared inside it.

lurleen

There's this wheeler Lurleen who despite her name is a lot more popular than me. Popular kids will sometimes talk to her if no one else is looking. Normal kids will push her if she's lagging behind. I'm late for class every day.

I sometimes want someone to push me but at the same time I know I'd be offended if they did. I'm independent and I'm not pathetic but that's different from being a tree or a statue. Pushing a wheeler isn't just helping them, it's saying that despite being the way you are I recognize you, that what all those spokes are sticking out of is clearly human. People don't realize how much that means.

Even though the old man stole me ... Part of me feels grateful. He hasn't hurt me, he's scared me a lot. It's more attention than I've gotten in a long time. His stories are weird but like being read to. I've gotten used to falling asleep while he's talking, even though I'm never sure ...

If I'll ever wake up again.

A Thought Cloud

Y ou will never understand me. Don't even pretend to understand me. The best you can do is sit in an armchair too long till your legs go numb. Not being able to walk is the least part of being a wheeler. The chair is just furniture. It doesn't matter.

There's a thought cloud around me, of my own thoughts and other people's thoughts. There's what I think about me, and what I want to think, and what people think about me, and what they tell me they think. It's all different, it mixes together. It's a head storm, and all that blowing storming is what makes me a pretty complicated kid. *I* have trouble understanding me. So you better, too.

I Hate Myself

I guess I hate myself. I'm a snob because I hate myself. Being an advanced reader makes me pretty superior. Reading *David Copperfield*. If I liked myself I'd like other people and I wouldn't gaze down from my wheelchair like it was Castle Dracula.

I'd make a good writer. Most writers are snobs and failures. My cousin the writer is a snob and a failure. No one in my family hears of her books or reads them. She calls them goons, and swings her cape over her shoulder. She tilts her head even higher. She looks at the ceiling and walks into the wall. Even I hate her.

Most wheelers have high self-esteem. They can't help it because they're buried in shit. You're just so heroic, soldierly, unique. You have to mentally get out of your wheelchair and look down from the chandelier at you and your wheelchair covered in shit. Then you'll understand you aren't brave and so great because your legs don't work and you're pasted to a stupid chair. You're just a dumb metallic kid and your family steps

into you like a mine car and rides you down to hell.
They get to die then but you sit there in fire and suffer.

I'm a twelve-year-old kid.

Shit.

The Constipated Broccoli Kid

The old man gave me some cheese from his pocket. I don't generally eat cheese because it makes me constipated. Usually once a month I have a bowel crisis and my parents take me to St. James. This one time when he saw me coming, the fat orderly, he rolled his eyes and turned to the nurses and said: "Oh great, it's the constipated broccoli kid." Then the nurses all laughed. I could've died right there, so easily.

The cheese was covered in both mould and pocket fuzz. I ate it anyway. I was starving to death.

Caitlyn

It's beautiful out, today. It's crisp but it's sunny. I'm still wondering about that skeleton. I couldn't tell because the old man didn't stop but it looked like a femur and a ribcage.

A girl from town went missing. Caitlyn something. People formed search parties and looked for days but never found her. I always wondered what happened to her. It haunted me because she was my age.

Coyote or fox bones, probably.

The old man is curled up on the grass now, napping. He twitches a lot in his sleep. My aunt had a cat that slept in a vase and meowed to get out. Cats are perfect creatures, she'd say, as she shook it out of the vase like ketchup.

God, I feel so agitated.

Rachel

We used to have a maid, Rachel. I wasn't sure why I initially hated her, but I think it's because a maid is someone you pay to do the things you really should be doing yourself, and it makes you feel bad about yourself, so you treat them badly. I couldn't really treat her badly, but my parents treated her like shit. She looked forward to cleaning my room, I think, because I was usually in it, and my parents acted differently when I was around. Like if they raised their voices a thunderbolt might split me in half, and then they'd have *two* wheelchair daughters.

All I ever really wanted was for them to treat me like a real kid. To yell at me, punish me. When I looked at my dad with eyes that said: "*Dad*," he looked back with eyes that said: "May I help you to your room?" Or: "Can I be of any assistance?" Like I was a visiting aunt from Montana.

Rachel teased me and scolded me. I didn't like it at the time, I wasn't used to it, but thinking back ...

She read to me a few times. I'm a great reader, but some books are a challenge to hold open. Once I was reading, she was dusting something, I was really struggling with the binding, and she just snatched the book out of my hands and finished the chapter out loud. I was preparing to have a fit, but then surprisingly I liked listening. I missed it. She read to me a few more times, after that. Reading is a kind of love your parents give you and when they stop giving it there's just not as much love. It's like that with a lot of things, I guess. People really hug their small kids a lot. There's a little less love every day.

Dad fired Rachel last year. Not because of anything she did or said, even though whenever anything went missing he blamed her, then didn't apologize when it turned up under the couch, or behind the potted plant. It was just the recession and everything.

I miss Rachel, I guess. It's not like she was my Pegotty or anything. But when I read *David Copperfield* now, I read it in her voice, it's her voice in my brain telling me the story.

She was probably my only friend.

Whales

Whales could write great novels if they only had hands.

The Sea-Wave VI

Then I dreamed of a garden and woke in a garden. For I could hear the wind, still. In the green, grass. The stone changing, on which I lay, the cool stone ... to my lonesome bed. Believing ... I was still in that green place. For such a moment, only.

The moving grass. It could only be him. The dark man. Brother Ulgoth.

I listened. But heard nothing. And then *something*. So very, faintly. The tone, so familiar.

I rose. I approached the door. Observing the grille. There was no man there.

I stepped closer. Laying my hands on the bars, of the grille. Peering into the hall.

I saw only ... a shadow. And a deeper, shadow. The dark of the hall — there was a lone candle — and a greater shadow. The robe ... of this brother. The black robe. The back of it. He seemed ... to be speaking. Stirring, the black fabric of his hood. Surely, speaking. To the man in the cell, opposite.

I held, now, my ear, to the grille. And listened. As one might ... a tragic man, to a dark bird.

So gently speaking. So quiet, the hall, I could hear. I could hear, each word:

"The sea-wave comes and goes forever. It rushes against everything forever. Nothing, not iron, survives it. For the sea-wave flows forever. It takes away everything, forever. All crumbs, and the phantoms of all things. Until they're nothing. Everything, we have. The good things of earth. The miserable things. All suffering. All, is salt. Your bones. They will wash away. It will take them, the wave, away. The Earth itself, is salt, and will wash away. In the wave. For it comes and goes, forever."

Sliding my hand, down the wall. As a wave, against the wall. Falling.

An Ideal Secretary

You know, I don't hate the old man. He stole me, I am scared to death, I don't hate him. I don't know him or understand him. When a branch scratched me, he took a crust of bread out of his pocket and rubbed it on the scratch. At first I was appalled but ... Maybe he thought the mould was penicillin.

I'm not sure if what he's telling me is real-life stuff. It doesn't sound like anything I ever heard of happening to anyone.

I don't really know anyone.

Maybe he's illiterate and picked me as an ideal secretary who's quiet and works for bread crusts. His stories ... They could be life stories or a novel.

I don't know.

I'm writing it all down.

But I don't know.

The Fifth Dimension

When I wake up and I'm not in my room, I'm in the middle of nowhere, I'm cold and I'm in pain ...

It's like a dream.

One time ...

Mom was at Thee Lingerie. I was waiting outside, reading *David Copperfield*.

A woman came up to me. A smiling woman. She crouched down. She rubbed my shoulder. She whispered in my ear:

"It won't be like this in the Fifth Dimension."

She smiled even harder and squeezed my hand.

"In the Fifth Dimension, there is no disease. No *pain*. There is no suffering."

I looked down the aisles. I couldn't see my mom.

"Our spiritual bodies will be strong. We will *flourish*, all of us — and shine with the light of pure life."

I looked at her eyes. I hoped ... But she was. She *was* serious.

Sincerity is terrifying.

I felt like screaming.

The woman put something in my hand. A pamphlet. She kissed my cheek. Then she walked off, smiling.

When Mom came out of the store, I stuck the pamphlet in the front of *David Copperfield*. I pulled it out later, in my room.

Humankind will soon enter the Fifth Dimension, a dominion of Bliss and Serenity.

World peace, social harmony, copious joy. The Fifth Dimension sounded perfect.

Nothing perfect is real.

I ripped the pamphlet in half.

At the mall, I kept an eye out for the smiling lady. But I never saw her again. She probably got hospitalized or arrested. Or she took a strange turn and made it to the Fifth Dimension after all.

I took a strange turn, too.

If I saw her out *here*, the smiling woman ...

It wouldn't even surprise me.

The Minimalist

My grandpa's a minimalist. He takes medication. He just said: "I'm a minimalist" and got rid of his furniture. He sold his bed and sleeps on the couch. When we go there there's nowhere for anyone to sit but me. There's two empty rooms, a bathroom, and a mini fridge full of yogurt. My parents gave him a table but he threw it away. They sit with him on the floor and eat yogurt. My dad opened a cupboard once and a million silver yogurt lids tumbled out.

Mental illness is pretty common in my family.

Wilkins

My parents thought a pet would be good for me, so they bought me an insane cat I named Wilkins. The night before we picked him up at the humane society I pictured him hopping on my lap and being like a small friend.

There were a lot of cats at the humane society. I chose Wilkins because when I wheeled past he meowed instead of backing away. Plus his eyes were two different colours and sizes.

I loved Wilkins but every time he came up to me he'd scratch my legs like a scratching post. Then he'd look lovingly up at me with his crazed eyes while I sat there bleeding.

When my dad saw the marks on my legs he was horrified. My mom must've seen them when she was bathing me but she never said anything. Then I seemed to be allergic too, and for a while I needed an inhaler. So my parents took Wilkins back to the humane society. They said it might be just temporary. That was a couple years ago.

I miss Wilkins. He hurt me sometimes, but so did life. You can't take your life back to the humane society. Or I'd've tried that a long time ago.

Something

"See them?"

The old man stopped. He pointed at a tree.

I couldn't see anything.

"*See* them?" he said again, really looking at me. Really *talking* to me.

"*See?* You see?"

I shook my head.

He made a sound like a small dog and then pointed again but didn't say anything. Then he made a sound like a bigger dog. He crouched and walked around my chair. He was breathing, I could hear him making sounds at about my head level. His feet, or probably his knees, were scratching on the ground. Every minute or so my handlebars creaked, his breathing sounds moved from behind my back to just behind my left ear, it was like he was breathing in my ear. Then they move quickly back behind my chair and became whimper-y.

There was really nothing that I could see in the tree. There could've been a bird or a squirrel. Though I don't remember seeing one. It was just a big, I'd say, oak tree.

This went on for maybe an hour. Sometimes he was so quiet I wondered if he was falling asleep. I was getting sleepy. I almost fell asleep, or did fall asleep. But then he just sprang up and wheeled me on past the tree faster than I think I've ever been pushed. If I'd fallen out he probably would've crushed me to death. And kept going.

The Half-Kid

Once upon a time, I split in half. I tipped over and split in half. Then my mom picked up the half of me she didn't like and threw it down the well. The other half-kid's still up there looking down at me sometimes. Sometimes she goes away. I'm scared she might not ever come back. I'm lonely and I'm scared down here. When I see her for even a bit I'm so relieved. I stop having panic attacks. She looks at me sadly and I'm almost happy. But I want to scream be careful. And stay the fuck away from the edge.

Mrs. Ramshaw

Like most kids with no friends I've had imaginary friends. I used to have a cat and a friendly octopus but now I just have Mrs. Ramshaw. She's an old lady with swollen legs who I imagine lying in the guest bedroom, which is the next room down from mine. I've never really pictured her face, just her swollen legs projecting over the edge of the bed. I guess she's that tall.

I can't fall asleep without first thinking of Mrs. Ramshaw in the other room. I think of how old and sick she is, and how her fat legs stick out. It doesn't make sense but I only feel comfortable and okay if I know she's there. She doesn't say anything or do anything, just lies there breathing. My mom takes pink tranquillizers. Mrs. Ramshaw's legs are my pink tranquillizers. I just think of them sticking out and I drift to sleep.

I guess I try not to think about Mrs. Ramshaw's face because ... it might be my face. In the morning, when I wheel past the guest bedroom, I always check. I can't go by without checking. But I know if I ever really saw Mrs. Ramshaw lying there with my face I'd flop over dead. It's unhealthy, but ... That's always how I imagined I'd die.

Halloween

Every year to help me feel normal, my mom dresses me up as a cat or a lobster, and wheels me around the neighbourhood. She used to put on scarier costumes but I just wasn't into it. When you open the door and there's this sad kid kitten sitting there ... It's sort of cute and sad, like a puppy with three legs. But when it's a zombie in a chair, I watch their eyes, they are just genuinely horrified and sorry. They drop the licorice in the pail without smiling. Then slowly shut the door.

Last year I decided I didn't want to bother anymore, it was too much drama. I can't even eat hard candy. But my mom said she was worried I might become a shut-in and wrestled me into the lobster suit. She never dresses up as anything, she dresses as a neurotic mother. To express my disgust, I upset the candy pail skull, but then she put a string on the handle and around my back so I couldn't. So I put up with it. I just pretended to sleep. My hope was that people would think she was abusing me to get candy. Which wasn't too far from the truth.

Likes

I like Charles Dickens, I like Agatha Christie, I like Arthur Conan Doyle. I don't like Shakespeare yet but I think that I will. I like Lewis Carroll a lot, thought NOT *Sylvie and Bruno*. I like some things by Robert Lewis Stevenson, but not the early things. I like Ray Bradbury, but only the early things. There aren't many children's things I like. Children's writers write like they're desperate to be your friend, and you're wearing sunglasses that can't see desperation.

If I find time, I'd like to fall in love with poetry.

Meteors

Usually at night the old man stopped pushing me, but some nights he just kept on going. Looking up at the stars and not really watching where he was going. Sometimes as he was looking up he'd say Sirius or Vega or Polaris. He was actually pretty knowledgeable. I wondered if he'd been an astronomer or something. And why an astronomer would steal a wheelchair kid.

Normally when it got dark, though, he'd stop. He'd wheel me behind a bush or something and lie down beside me. If it was raining — well one time he took his jacket off and draped it over my head like I was a parakeet. I appreciated it but the odour was malevolent.

Only one time did he take me out of my chair and lay me on the ground. I was both nervous and refreshed. Because there were parts of my body, from sitting, that now felt like produce. But when a really strange person who stole you lays you down in the bushes, if you don't get nervous, you're demented. He just lay me down, though, and lay down beside me. He didn't do anything or say anything. Then he pointed up.

It was a meteor shower. I'd never seen one. It was basically streaks of dust. The dust glowed brightly for a bit, then disappeared. There was maybe one meteor every thirty seconds. They would've been high in the atmosphere, but it seemed like if you reached out, you could feel the dust on your fingers. I had to stop myself from trying.

After about a half hour, the old man lifted me back into my chair. Then he lay down in the dirt and went to sleep.

It really wasn't much of a meteor shower. More of a meteor dew.

Pretty much everything is disappointing.

The Sea-Wave VII

It happened.

The sound of thunder, of water. Before I could rise from my bed, it lifted. It was taken, by the wave.

With so much violence, I was thrown. Striking the door of my prison. I cried out, then, rising in water, trying the door. My eye level with the grille. I looked through it, and a man looked through, wildly. Water poured over him, and flowed now, through the grille. He rushed away. I thrust ... my fingers ... through the grille. Through it, I could see, dimly, men. Running.

I did not know how fast the water rose. My head touched the stone ceiling. There was nothing, onto which to hold. Only my life. For a moment, only, of more life, I would hold my breath. I would wait, until it reached ... the scar, on my ear. My final breath, would be the film of air, on the water. I would draw it off, the film, and hold it, holding closed my eyes.

More thunder. The *door*. It broke open. Crashing against the wall. There was a rushing, a suction. It pulled me deep underwater, through the door. Into the hall.

I struck my head, on the wall. Men were running. I rose, choking. I rose and fell again. I had breathed in water, and burned. As I stood burning, the wave came against me, again, and broke me. I struck the wall again. I was pinned, by water, on stone. It was very nearly to my knees, the water. It was rushing from the door. It was cold, and burning.

At the end of the hall was a staircase, of stone. Everywhere, men were running. Men ... were beating, the sealed doors. Terrible, their rhythm, in my ears.

Candles, in their iron stands, were lifting and ... extinguishing.

Men were running.

There was somewhere, a staircase.

I pulled away from the wave. I somehow ... escaped it. I felt along the wall. My head in pain. The water reached my knees.

I could see nothing.

Paw-Paw

When Tay-Lin went to India, we looked after her eclectus Paw-Paw.

Mom put the cage in the living room so the bird could observe our dysfunction.

Dad tried coaxing Paw-Paw to talk. She still just squawked after a week but he didn't give up. I'm not sure ... I don't remember him ever spending that much time with me.

Feeding Paw-Paw was my job. Pineapple, strawberries. Grapefruit, she spat back out. We had that in common.

I hadn't realized I could be nurturing.

One morning between bites of pineapple, Paw-Paw said: "I love you."

I'd underestimated her.

Paw-Paw cocked her head. She looked at me like she expected a reply.

She'd overestimated me.

"I love you," she said again.

My parents love me. They used to tell me. I have a good memory.

I don't know why but I opened the cage and Paw-Paw flew around the living room, shitting everywhere and squawking.

When Mom came out of the kitchen with more fruit, she swore. Paw-Paw kept repeating: "Shit."

Mom grounded me for a week — a meaningless gesture.

After dinner, Dad went to the living room. Mom gave me sorbet and complained about her depression. "Life is medieval," she said.

When I wheeled through the living room, after, Dad was feeding Paw-Paw. So I didn't have to. I went into the elevator.

"I love you," I heard him say, over and over, as the door closed.

Rose Bush

There's a rose bush under my window, a dead one, that Mom used to threaten to rip up but forgot about. When I'm upset, I drop things vengefully into it. Hairbrushes, cutlery, artwork. Anything that frustrates me. If my parents have ever seen the crumpled up paper and sweaters sticking out of the rose bush, they haven't made it a part of their conversation.

They enrage me more than anything. I sometimes picture their legs poking out of the rose bush, thrashing for a minute, then going soft. It's not healthy. But it helps.

X-Rays

People can be tough to figure out. I've figured out a lot of people, I've got x-rays, but there's a few you just can't fathom. They've got the lead vest on from the dentist. If you want to be a mystery you can keep your hands exposed and your head. You only have to cover your heart.

It's strange because I'm not scared of the old man but I'm nervous, I'm unsure of him. I've thought about him *a lot*. I'm the bird looking down at us from a million points of view. And I still don't get it. I'm a smart kid. But I like the kinds of problems I can solve.

I just don't *get* it.

Naked Dad

Mom shook me awake in the night.

"Your father wants to see you."

The elevator door opened. The living room was full of people. It was like a birthday party only no one was speaking, just sitting there staring at my dad, who was sitting in the middle of the couch, naked. Then everyone stared as Mom wheeled me in front of him like a birthday cake. Before I could close my eyes, Dad jumped up and tried squeezing behind the TV but his butt was too big. He said something to my mom and she picked up the phone and called more and more people.

When our neighbour Macey got there she took one look and called an ambulance, though my mom objected. She didn't want to make a fuss.

When the ambulance guys came, they convinced Dad to put his shorts back on and go peacefully with them. They kept him in the hospital overnight. When he came home, he seemed fine if slightly dazed.

No one ever mentioned this again.

Creakle

Once to cheer me up my mom bought me an octopus in a wheelchair. Two of its arms were pushing the wheels, four were on the leg rests, and two were raised up in the air like it was a solid thrill to be an octopus in a wheelchair. It was cute but an octopus is basically a monster and this may be the wrong kind of metaphor to hurl at your disabled child.

I named the octopus Creakle because it sounded Dickensian.

I slept with Creakle for a week. Then I dropped him in the rose bush.

For all I know, he's still there.

School

M y school has a zero tolerance policy for bullying.
If you tell someone you're being bullied, they're re-
quired to look up from their cellphone briefly.

I've been hurting for a long time now. When someone hurts you, you become their victim. It's what you
are. Our school is full of victims, usually the brightest,
most talented kids. We are the emotionally damaged
future. When someone hurts you it knocks a piece out
of you until one day you just fall to pieces. It takes a
long time. Everyone sees it happen. The teachers see it.
I guess it's easy watching someone else's kids being
eaten, like the maggoty kids on Third World commer-
cials.

It just doesn't pay to care.

The Sad Kid

You are going to die in this chair.

Thoughts get stuck in my brain like gum.

I don't think anything negative when I'm reading. I guess that's why I read so much. I have to keep my brain cells as busy as I can. Or I just wouldn't be able to live.

I'm not sure if I was born sad or if it's just because of my life.

I should probably be on drugs.

I Don't Want to Grow Up

I don't want to grow up.

Home Life of the Victorians

My aunty gave me a book called *Home Life of the Victorians*. It was 100+ colour plates of Victorians doing Victorian things like playing the harpsichord and smiling gaily. They seemed pretty happy despite TB.

I tried picturing myself sitting next to the Victorians but every time one of the smiling ladies got up quickly and wheeled me out of the frame. Then went back to her needlework.

The book was a nice thought and probably expensive.

I dropped it in the rose bush.

Run

When I opened my eyes, the old man was leaning on a tree. He was sitting with his knees up, leaning, with his arms around it and his head against it, hugging it.

He was crying. He was quiet, but he was crying. There was a dark line running down the bark.

The old man looked a hundred. He looked like a kid.

If god had decided to wake up and stuck a hand in me and I stood up, I wouldn't've run. I would've stepped out of my chair, gone over to the old man, crouched down and hugged him. I wouldn't've said anything. But I'd've hugged him for a long time.

Then I would've run.

The Sea-Wave VIII

I was then ... in the ocean. Water flowed over me. It seemed — yet it was not a wave. It was a fold, only. It was not even, the ocean. It was ...

I lay in confusion. In a quiet room. The white sheet lay next to me. My bed was the ocean. There were other beds, like other small oceans, and men in them. They were so close together, the beds, end to end, along two walls of a long room. Few men could have passed between them.

A door. At one end of the room. For so long I watched it, not even thinking. It was difficult, thinking. So I rested. And looked again. I looked, only there was no door. There was only ... a shadow.

And then a woman came in, like a wave. Her uniform, white. Her skin. She held something.

She approached one man. She bent over him. I could hear, something. Some gentle tone.

She moved on. The next, and the next man. One man *screamed*. He lifted his arms. In an instant, he was calm, again. And said nothing.

She was so close, now. This bright woman. Turning sideways, she sidled between the beds. As white, it seemed, and as thin, as a ream of paper.

And she was above me. Her face ... was strange. Unsmiling. She held a syringe. She lifted my arm. It was so pale, and thin, I did not think it was my arm. It was some other man's. She lifted water. I had the strength of water. I did not resist. I did not even feel the syringe.

Then the room was moving. The man next to me, was now ... above me. His bed was above me, and above me again. When I moved my head, the beds went with it. The walls did not stop them. They remained in the air ... then disappeared.

She passed my bed again, the woman. She moved toward the door. The door was still open, yet ... There was a pile of men, before it. They had lain down, one on another, to stop her. To block her way. They lay completely still. They did not even seem to be breathe.

She moved closer, the woman. She approached the door and the men, not slowing. She moved *through* them. Then closed the door.

I lay back in the ocean.

I could hear the ocean.

Every Day

Every day is a somewhat new day.

Macey

Our one neighbour Macey is super-Christian. She squeezes through keyholes. I don't think Mom even likes her, but you can't tell someone who wears a shawl to go away.

When Macey mentions Jesus, she can't stop. Like the kid in Grade 10 who says "fuck" uncontrollably. If Mom tries to distract her by talking about dish detergent or her new moustache trimmer, Macey will say something like "Jesus had a moustache," with a dreaming look in her eyes like she's remembering her dead husband.

When Mom leaves the room to get coffee or use the bathroom, I'm terrified. Macey usually ignores me but when we're alone she talks to me in a strange quiet voice, like she's trying to hypnotize someone who's sleeping. She always says more or less the same thing: that Jesus loves us all or that no matter how badly off we think we are there's always millions of people who are worse off and if we could all just rejoice in that and love Jesus we'd be so happy.

I thought about this and tried doing it but picturing millions of suffering kids didn't boost my mood a bit. Neither did a dying guy pinned to a stick.

Only one thing did make me happier: imagining Macey on an adjacent cross with blood gushing out of her hands and feet.

I'm not worried about going to hell. I've lived there a long time already.

Music

I used to feel emotion all the time. I wasn't quite happy, but I didn't realize how unhappy I was. Once you understand that, you just can't go back. You can try, but you can't go back.

When I hear music ... I can listen to music for hours sometimes and nothing happens. But then I'll wake up in the night, I sleep with my radio on, and I'll hear a song that wakes me up *again*.

It's amazing. Like remembering my name. Everything is so clear and so real again. It's like I can breathe again. It's just the best feeling. I wonder, *Do other people feel like that all the time?*

When I wake up, it's gone.

Red Hands

The old man has red hands. The outsides of his hands are red from the sun but his palms are even redder and cooked-looking. At first I wondered why but then I realized he's stopping a lot to pull out the weeds that keep choking up my wheels and it's wrecking his hands. There's streaks of green on them and brown dots that are probably blood. There's a guy named Gerry who my dad says was an ordinary working guy until his brain came out. We saw him at the mall. He paced a lot and occasionally started laughing insanely and rubbing his face. His face and his hands were red and raw. My dad asked him how he was and he just laughed and rubbed his face off. Then his mom took him to the bathroom. Then my mom took me to the bathroom and I threw up.

Abilities Camp

Abilities Camp sounded fun. I was glad to get away. There were a few wheelers sitting outside, so I loosely associated with them until my parents drove away. Then we wheeled into the auditorium.

I'd never seen so many sick kids. The girl next to me ... She was just a head in a chair. I sat around until the lights went mostly out. Then the fat lady licked her microphone and said dramatically: "We are *not* disabled. We are *multitalented*." And everyone cheered, who was able.

When the lights came back on, I looked around. The head in the chair was staring at me. This other girl was struggling with her nebulizer.

I never really realized I was a freak until someone made a camp for it.

Smudge

In my dreams I have a wheelchair. Every time. Other kids are playing ring-toss with unicorns and I'm wheeling along, looking for ramp access.

One time on AM 800 CHAD this dream expert was talking about either lucid or lucent dreams. The idea is you're dreaming, you *realize* you're dreaming, you *take control* of your dreams. Then you really could if you wanted toss those rings, or eat the mayor, or pretty much anything else you could think of.

So I tried it. Just before I fell asleep, I told myself I was going to have — I think it was a lucid dream. The trouble is when you're dreaming, you can't *tell* you're dreaming. So if you've got a baby growing on your kneecap, your brain just says: "Yup. As usual." You're supposed to insert a clue into your dream before you nod off and when you run into that clue you'll know you're asleep. In my dreams I'm usually just quietly reading, so my dream clue was that I'd read the word "smudge," which is my least favourite word in English and the first word that terrible poets reach for when they're trying hard to be metaphorical.

So I kept thinking smudge, smudge, getting sleepier and sleepier, and when I dreamed I was reading I *saw* the smudge, and had an epiphany. I threw my book down. "I'm dreaming," I said to myself. "This is all a dream. I'm *taking control* of my dreams. I'm going ... to fly." Flying, just the freeness of it, is probably the ultimate wheeler fantasy.

I closed my eyes. I *focused*.

And then it happened.

I felt myself rising higher and higher. I got that butterfly feeling. It should have been so amazing.

But it wasn't amazing. It was fucking depressing. Because my wheelchair just floated up with me. No matter how hard I rocked or pushed down on my armrests, it stuck to me. And I felt so much sadder and more devastated than I've ever felt in my waking life.

I floated back down to the ground. I picked up my book and I kept on reading.

Then I woke up.

Drawing

I should probably draw a picture of the old man. If I get recalled to life again people will want to know who to look for. Or if they just find a skeleton with a memorandum book.

Drawing isn't my forte. I draw a lot. A couple months back I drew a picture of a hermit crab out of the encyclopaedia and even though I don't really like people to see my work I was proud enough, it even looked like a crab, to stick it on the fridge. No one said anything till the Jehovah lady came. My mom lets them in because she can only disappoint family members. They went into the kitchen. I listened from the top of the stairs. The lady must've seen the drawing because she said: "Oh how old is your little one?" There was a long pause, then mom said: "Twelve." Then a longer pause where I imagined the Jehovah lady screwing up her corneas and maybe slanting her head like a puppy. "Oh," she said, finally. Then she started in about Jehovah. I retracted back into my room like the nearest seashell.

I guess with my skill a drawing would be worthless.
And there's no point again because the old man looks
exactly like da Vinci's self-portrait.

It's uncanny.

Dentistry

I bit the dentist. If you gouge your hook into my cavity and ask me if it hurts I'm going to bite you. Like the crocodile in *Peter Pan*. My main virtue may be my strong teeth.

I get my dentistry done now at the hospital. They put you under and after you can't have solid food or your lungs will collapse. The doctor illustrated this by drawing eyes on a sandwich bag, then blowing it up and popping it on his chest. At the same time as the *pop* the nurse jammed the IV in. The last thing I remember is the doctor crumpling the puppet with its head blown open.

I couldn't eat for three days. I could have broth but chose not to. Not snacking is murder. I wanted some mixed nuts but kept imagining my chest flattening like the card guys in *Alice's Adventures*. Or my head blowing open.

On the fourth day I ate breakfast and threw up. "Life is simpler," my mom said as she wiped it up, "when you don't bite people."

She's probably right.

Symphony Under the Stars

I couldn't believe what was happening. I'd been out so long and away from everything. I thought maybe I was going crazy.

I woke up. It was nighttime. You could hardly see anything but the old man was still moving. It felt like he was pushing me uphill because of the pressure of my head against the headrest.

I closed my eyes again. I couldn't see anything. The pushing got slower as the hill got steeper. The old man was really puffing. I was worried he'd drop dead, then I'd roll back over him and tip over. There might be coyotes.

I heard something. It got louder as we went along. It sounded like music — *but it couldn't be music.* I hadn't had much water or sleep. *A hallucination.*

It sounded like Handel or Mozart. Then I was sure it was Mozart. It was a divertimento. I have a CD of divertimentos.

There were lights on the other side of the hill. The old man slowed down but kept pushing me. The music got louder as the lights got brighter. It was like there was a crown on top of the hill. Then we were on top of the crown.

For a minute I thought I was dead though I'm not Christian. I'd been moving to the light and there was music. And then all these people. There were maybe five hundred people sitting and standing at the bottom of the hill. It was like a small valley filled with people. There was a symphony on a stage. The lights were shining on a banner that read: "SYMPHONY UNDER THE STARS." My parents had taken me to something like this years ago, maybe even in this same spot. For a while they thought it was important to nourish my brain.

It was so amazing to hear music again I almost cried. I was so thirsty and this was as good as water.

The old man stopped pushing me. I think he was listening to the music. He stepped up to a tree. He put his arms around it and looked down at the lights and the people. Then he sat in the grass and looked and listened. He put his head back like he was in ecstasy.

We sat there for close to an hour. They played Schubert and a few movie themes. Then everyone clapped and started walking away. The musicians packed up their instruments. The conductor held his hand above his eyes and looked up at us almost like he could see something. Then he turned and walked away with the rest.

The old man jumped up and pushed me down the side of the hill into a new area of darkness.

I wondered ...

Will I ever hear music again?

Dream

I can't forget. Your memory helps you but it kills you too. It picks you up and it drops you. It's your depressed mom who loves you and wishes you were dead.

My mom gets me into my chair. I sleep with my head at the foot of the bed so it's easier for her, my dad leaves early, to pull me straight back into my chair. When your mom's grunting under you, you can't forget you're a flour bag. When you move your hand and it doesn't move how you *need* it to. When you rest it on your armrest, press a button. Everything reminds you.

But I want to forget. I want to lay back in the grass and not think about the million strands of grass, but just *relax*. I want that so bad. It's a dream, it keeps me going. If I could forget for just a minute. It's sad but it's my dream.

It's better than nothing.

The Sea-Wave IX

Years, appeared. They merely appeared. I lay them ...
on the table. And counted them.

I have my freedom.

But I did not have my freedom.

When you are imprisoned, it is your skin, and *some
other thing*, which are imprisoned. A small thing: a particle. There are so many elements in a chemical. Remove
one, and it is some other thing. It is not the chemical.
It is nothing.

I now had my freedom. But I wanted *a particle*. The
other thing. It remained in prison. Lying, by the next
condemned man. As a facing page.

It will lie there, forever.

The Sad Fly

Just thinking about my mom … I've thrown up before. She's not what you'd call motherly. She never really held me. I've heard her say: "I'm not a baby person." But you *had* a baby, Mom. I imagine her reading magazines, and my dad holding me, looking worried and sad.

No one holds me now. I sit in my corner. Mom reads magazines, Dad sits attached to his paper, like a sad fly.

I don't think having a damaged kid really killed my mom. But it *murdered* my dad. He's never said that, but …

I can tell.

Observation

My one hobby is observation. I wheel right up to the margin till my feet touch the red line and I sit there and stare. I make my observations, I write them down. When you're old especially, life has to be just an album of observations; you turn the pages all day until your arthritis aches. When you're a wheeler, that's really all life is, too. You've gotta hold onto things or you'll have nothing. And you already have so little.

Conversation

The point of conversation is to stop a person's words from ever getting out of their mouth. Someone talking is that foam sealant that keeps the listening person's words from leaking out. If they do get out, maybe there was too much space between your words, you have to cut them off like sausages and cram them back in. If the person talks about their new business, you tell them how it's so very likely in today's economy to fail. You push the words down their throat past the epiglottis until they choke to death. Then you go on talking.

Walking-Stick

The old man has a tattoo on his forearm. Something with claws, a lion or a dragon. He rolled his sleeves up when I thought he was going to try climbing this dead tree. But he just pushed on it like he wanted to topple it. It was dead but not dead enough. He gave up.

He pushed me for a while, then stopped at another tree. There were a lot of white dead trees in this area which I think comes from flooding. This one went down easy. It smashed on the ground and bits of branches went everywhere. One scratched me on the cheek hard. I touched it but there wasn't any blood.

I watched the old man picking up branches and dropping them for a long time. He picked up one long one and whacked it on the ground till the fragile bits snapped off. Then he tested his weight on it. I assumed he wanted a walking-stick. Though he hasn't used it yet. He just rests it across my handlebars and holds onto it and pushes me at the same time.

I'm not sure what he's up to.

The Glass Jar

The glass jar my mom throws pennies in plays the wedding waltz when you open it. You just have to wind a key in the lid. When I was younger, when my mom rolled her pennies, it was my job to wind up the jar. When I heard the wedding waltz I knew my presence was needed. It made me feel needed. It was something I could do usually without help. It was important. Small things keep you going.

Over time the jar stopped working. The music got so slow it was chilling. I'd feel suspense. I'd imagine skeletons dancing. My parents seemed happier when they were younger.

Once when I wound the jar it went *clank* and died. "Look what you've done," Mom said. She didn't need me after that. She rolls the pennies herself now, in silence.

But sometimes when she opens the jar it still makes one *ding* like a last gasp of romance. I can hear it even from my room. It reminds me of how things were. I used to — I'd get so sad. I'd close my eyes for a long time. But not anymore.

I stopped winding my heart up a long time ago.

Shining Star

She's our shining star. We love her. The disease has stolen her. It's taken her away. But ... we can still see, if we look closely, in her eyes ... that old sparkle. She smiles. In some tunnel of her mind, she's smiling.

She's our shining star. We love her.

Jane

I have an auntie who's — most people would say — retarded. Everyone calls her Janey, though I think of her as Jane, because Janey just makes her sound cuter than she really is. Because she is basically a shakey, wired lady with a moustache. She has glasses, but she doesn't look through her glasses. She looks over them, and her eyeballs are meatballs and terrifying. Her ordinary voice is screaming.

Jane is Mom's sister so she materializes at times. They can't stand each other but guilt is the staple gun that holds families together. I hate going anywhere or being seen with Jane because I know what people are thinking. They're looking at the two of us, and then at my parents, and thinking: Whoa, imagine being stuck with one of those, AND one of *those*. Their hearts must be like ripped-apart flags. We can now be pretty happy by contrast, and have those ice-cream sandwiches after all. Also, they probably think we're both retarded, and that it's one of those fun outings that retarded people are made to take at strip malls and smaller parks.

Jane lives alone but shouldn't. Mom said she has the IQ of maybe a four- or a five-year-old. There aren't many four- or five-year-olds who have their own apartment, plus a cat, with cat shit all over everything, and burned-black pots and pans in the trash can.

I overheard Mom say: "My life would be simpler if Janey didn't exist."

I overheard Dad say: "Shh."

Bodyguard

I hate my face. My nose looks like it broke off a statue and got pasted on in a hurry. My one eye is higher than the other. They had to pry me out of my mom with pliers. The regular forceps didn't work so someone had to get special forceps from the basement. Your skull is taffy when you're born and if they stretch it they're scared to push it back. If they'd known how I was going to turn out, they maybe would've cared less and pressed in the dents with their thumbs.

Compared to Jay Kwan, I got off easy. The one side of his skull is twisted up. His left eye is up in his hair. When I first saw him I wanted to cry. Also he was cute, he would've been so cute, if it weren't for his tragic deformity. He's weirdly popular. His girlfriend is normal and volatile. I don't think anyone would tease her — or him, either — or she'd just erupt. She's like his crazed bodyguard, which is just what a disabled kid needs in their life. Or they'll never make it.

Helen

Sometimes the old man says what sounds like "Helen" just under his breath, which considering how bent over he is is practically right in my ear. It's unsettling waking up with this raspy "Helen" in my ear like a wasp. Once he shouted "Helen" when he woke up then he ran to me. I'm not sure if he thinks my name is Helen, or ... He could have me confused with someone else, which would make this whole thing a dumb mix-up.

I don't even look like a Helen.

The Sea-Wave X

Whenever ... I was joyful (I was so seldom joyful), there would be a voice. In my ear. A soft voice. A voice like the water. It would change, as water changes. But the words. They did not change. *The words.* They were always the same.

"The sea-wave comes and goes forever. It rushes against everything forever. Nothing, not iron, survives it. For the sea-wave flows forever. It takes away everything, forever. All crumbs, and the phantoms of all things. Until they're nothing. Everything, we have. The good things of earth. The miserable things. All suffering. All, is salt. Your bones. They will wash away. It will take them, the wave, away. The Earth itself, is salt, and will wash away. In the wave. For it comes and goes, forever."

And there would be no more joy.

Sunburn

My hands are so burnt now they're not hands. They're tongues.

I've never had a tan. There are gross old celebrities who resemble smoked fish because they think if they hide under a tan we won't notice they're three-quarters dead. I feel like one now.

I need my sunglasses. I have a small hole in my one cornea from looking at the sun too much when I was younger. I remember once my auntie said to me: "What are you doing?" I was staring at the sun. "Don't do that," she said. I kept doing it. "Do you want to be *blind* too, kid?" she said, turning my wheelchair around. Later, I bit her thumb.

I'm nervous. It's the part of the movie where you know something big has to happen because there's only ten minutes left.

The trees are getting thicker.

My red hands are burning and shaking.

I almost wish I was home.

The Sun

I like looking out the window, I liked to, in my room. There wasn't much to see. But I still liked to.

I saw my parents walking home. They didn't see me. The looked heartbroken. Like plants that hadn't been watered. I know they want to do the normal family stuff but most normal family places don't have a wheelchair lift or the right accessories. When people ask them in a confidential voice how they're doing they put on their smiles and then after peel them off like a sunburn.

I guess I'm the sun.

One Rotund Tragedy

My life has been one rotund tragedy. It's sad. There are so many things that *can* go right, but sometimes they all flop over like they smelled gas. My mom had maybe a kindergarten of miscarriages. They were all me's that gave it their pathetic best but couldn't quite make a go of it. And then I gave it my equally pathetic best but for some reason just barely made it. I sometimes wonder if my embryo had just smothered itself in egg yolk like the others if things would have turned out so much better for everyone. My parents would've bought a dog.

David Copperfield is good but not so good that you'd sit in acid reading it.

It's almost that good.

Something

He sometimes makes these beast sounds. It's this throat-whistling like a dog that's struggling to get comfortable. I'd say he's nervous or in pain. Maybe if you get nervous enough and hurt bad enough you lose it.

This all makes sense to him, I guess. It *means* something. Hopefully it does because my own life has been meaningless. I haven't been anything to anyone.

But to the old man ...

It's sad, but I guess I might be something.

Green Acres

I could barely see it in the moonlight but I'm pretty sure the sign I scratched my arm against read: "GREEN ACRES."

Green Acres looked much more like a large, dark forest. When it comes to children entering forests, good things don't generally happen.

The second time I fell out of my chair, I hit my head on a tree trunk. I didn't hit it that hard but ... My brain is the only thing I have going for me. I wouldn't mind, really, being a brain in a jar. As long as I could still read *David Copperfield.*

I couldn't see anything in the forest. All I could hear was the squealing of my wheels and the crunchy cereal things they were crushing. All I could think of was the birds and squirrels leaning out of their tree holes and staring. What they were probably thinking was "better her than us."

The old man slowed down a bit.

He stopped.

There was some kind of building just ahead. It had a doorway but no door. The old man pushed me through it.

It was black inside. The old man wheeled me a few feet then turned me around so I faced the door hole.

There was a clunk like he'd thrown down his walking stick. Then a crunch like he was lying down in leaves. Pretty soon he was snoring.

I stared at the doorway for a long time. When the moon went behind a cloud, the doorway disappeared.

I'm never going to see anyone ever again.

Again

When I woke up at dawn, I was lying on the floor beside my wheelchair.

It was an old shack full of leaves.

The old man was gone. So was his stick.

A raccoon ran out of the room.

I squirmed a bit and got my memorandum book out of the side pouch and a pen.

I wrote until I passed out.

When I woke up, I was in my chair and the chair was moving. My memorandum book was on my lap. I kept tipping forward and almost falling out and the old man kept stopping and pulling me back.

I held on tight to my memorandum book.

I passed out again.

The Sea-Wave XI

But nothing in life surprises. Truly. Not even ... the extraordinary thing. It is only a page. One page. There will still be another, and another. A thrilling page, an awful. They will all, as stems of grass, bend over. For our poet lies dreaming. With his dreaming book. On the green lawn. It lays ... on his breastbone, open. The book. And the wind — *he is dreaming* — takes his words away. They turn to ash seed. And they blow away.

So Much

There's so much to live for.
I just haven't figured out what.

The Sea-Wave XII

I have prayed this living was a dream.
   I have even prayed.

Collapse

He was pushing me slowly. It was so windy.

A leaf fell in my hair.

The old man fell.

I thought he was running. I moved so fast. He was falling.

My chair tipped back and slammed hard on the ground. My head slid back off my headrest over I think his walking-stick. The old man's face slammed right onto my face. My nose fit right between his nose and his lips. His breath fogged up my glasses and smelled like death. I could only see fog.

Then I felt his one hand sliding down my arm. He was maybe trying to grab my hand. But then he just stopped moving.

He made a soft noise.

Then my glasses unfogged.

Black Hole

The old man's throat is a black hole.

When I look down, I can see his eyes.

I try not to look down.

I moved my head back and forth until his head fell off me and onto the ground beside me. Then I reached for my memorandum book.

There's still a few pages left.

The End of the Story

This wasn't what I pictured. When I pictured the end of the story.

It's the end of the story.

I haven't been okay in a long time. I've been hurting for a long, long time. When you're suffering ...

Suffering ends. One way or the other.

It had to happen.

It's happening.

leaves

You think of things differently. You do. You can be sad when you're dying, but you can't hate yourself. You're barely there. You can't hate vapour or a rare mineral. Whoever you were isn't there.

I'm turning to leaves. It feels like. I feel so light.

I'll turn to leaves.

Then I'll blow away.

Mom, Dad

...

Pain

I'm in so much pain.
My stomach hurts bad.
My heart broke.

Untitled

I can hear the ocean.
I don't know where I am.

Acknowledgements

Extracts from *The Sea-Wave* were first published in *The Walrus* (online), *Broken Pencil*, *Word Riot* and *Writing Tomorrow*. My thanks to the editors. Thanks to Guernica, too.

About the Author

Rolli is a writer, illustrator and cartoonist from Regina, SK, Canada. He's the author of two short story collections (*I Am Currently Working On a Novel* and *God's Autobio*), two collections of poems (*Mavor's Bones* and *Plum Stuff*) and two children's titles (*Kabungo* and *Dr. Franklin's Staticy Cat*). His cartoons appear regularly in *The Wall Street Journal*, *Reader's Digest*, *Harvard Business Review*, *The Walrus*, *Adbusters* and other popular outlets. Visit Rolli's website (rollistuff.com) and follow him on Twitter @rolliwrites.

MARQUIS

Québec, Canada

RECYCLED
Paper made from
recycled material
FSC® C103567

Printed on Enviro 100% post-consumer EcoLogo certified paper,
processed chlorine free and manufactured using biogas energy.